SHOES FROM GRANDPA

by MEM FOX • Illustrated by PATRICIA MULLINS

SCHOLASTIC INC.

New York Toronto London Auckland Sydney

LATE one summer Jessie's father
invited all the family over for a barbecue.

When Grandpa saw Jessie he stood back and said,
"My, how you've grown! You'll need a new pair
of shoes this winter, and I'll buy them."

5

"Thanks a lot, Grandpa," said Jessie.

Then her dad said,
"I'll buy you some socks from the local shops,
to go with the shoes from Grandpa."

And her mom said,
"I'll buy you a skirt that won't show the dirt,
to go with the socks from the local shops,
to go with the shoes from Grandpa."

And her cousin said,
"I'll look for a blouse with ribbons and bows,
to go with the skirt that won't show the dirt,
to go with the socks from the local shops,
to go with the shoes from Grandpa."

And her sister said,
"I'll get you a sweater when the weather gets wetter,
to go with the blouse with ribbons and bows,
to go with the skirt that won't show the dirt,
to go with the socks from the local shops,
to go with the shoes from Grandpa."

And her grandma said,
"I'll find you a coat you could wear on a boat,
to go with the sweater when the weather gets wetter,
to go with the blouse with ribbons and bows,
to go with the skirt that won't show the dirt,
to go with the socks from the local shops,
to go with the shoes from Grandpa."

And her aunt said,
"I'll knit you a scarf that'll make us all laugh,
to go with the coat you could wear on a boat,
to go with the sweater when the weather gets wetter,
to go with the blouse with ribbons and bows,

to go with the skirt that won't show the dirt,
to go with the socks from the local shops,
to go with the shoes from Grandpa."

And her brother said,
"I'll find you a hat you can put on like that,
to go with the scarf that'll make us all laugh,
to go with the coat you could wear on a boat,
to go with the sweater when the weather gets wetter,
to go with the blouse with ribbons and bows,
to go with the skirt that won't show the dirt,
to go with the socks from the local shops,
to go with the shoes from Grandpa."

And her uncle said,
"I'll buy you some mittens that are softer than kittens,
to go with the hat you can put on like that,
to go with the scarf that'll make us all laugh,
to go with the coat you could wear on a boat,

to go with the sweater when the weather gets wetter,
to go with the blouse with ribbons and bows,
to go with the skirt that won't show the dirt,
to go with the socks from the local shops,
to go with the shoes from Grandpa.''

And Jessie said,
"You're all so kind that I hate to be mean,
but please, would one of you buy me some jeans?"

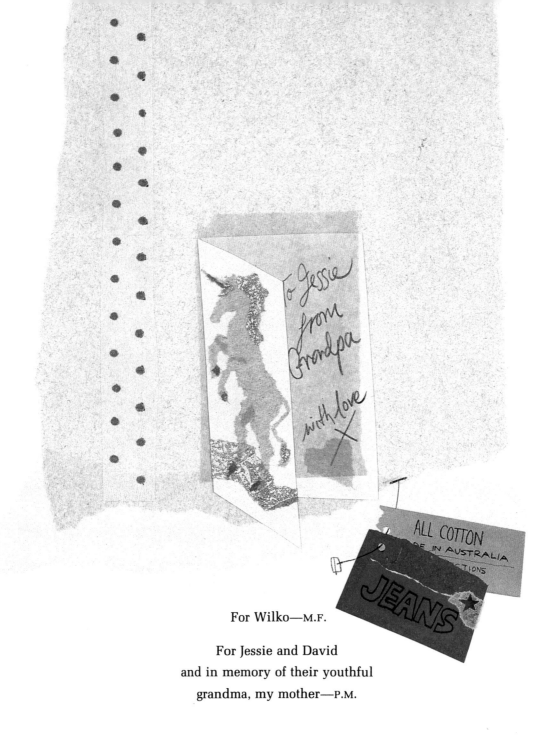

For Wilko—M.F.

For Jessie and David
and in memory of their youthful
grandma, my mother—P.M.

Text copyright © 1989 by Mem Fox.
Illustrations copyright © 1989 by Patricia Mullins.
All rights reserved. Published by Scholastic Inc., 555 Broadway,
New York, NY 10012, by arrangement with Orchard Books.
Book Design by Mina Greenstein.
The text of this book is set in 16 pt. Melior.
The illustrations are torn-paper collage, reproduced in full color.
Printed in the U.S.A.
ISBN 0-590-60349-3

2   3   4   5   6   7   8   9   10   14   02   01   00   99   98   97   96